Tree in the Trail

Tree in the Trail

WRITTEN AND ILLUSTRATED BY

Holling Clancy Holling

HOUGHTON MIFFLIN COMPANY   BOSTON

Acknowledgment

I wɪsʜ to thank my wife, Lucille Webster Holling, for her help in completing the illustrations in this book; her many hours of research on the trail of obscure data have contributed greatly to authoritative detail, and she designed the color map.

I also wish to thank Mr. Arthur Woodward, Director of History and Anthropology of the Los Angeles Museum, for certain data on costume and armament of the Spanish Southwest; and for details of a Conestoga wagon, early prototype of those used on the Santa Fe Trail.

THE AUTHOR

Contents

1. THE LONE SAPLING

An Indian boy and his uncle, a scout of the Kansas tribe, followed an ancient buffalo trail up a low hill. Two rocky buttes of the same size stood on the hilltop, a large pond between them. The boy raced toward this pond, but his uncle cried 'that is the buffalo's muddy watering place. We'll drink from the spring above it.' And so they drank clear, cold water bubbling from the rocky side of one butte.

The scout climbed the butte to stand motionless on its flat top. His keen eyes searched the Great Plains below him. Tall grass billowed in the wind like waves on an endless sea. Tiny dots moved in the distance, on the trail over which they had come.

The boy explored the shores of the pond. Among scattered rocks stood a single cottonwood sapling, no taller than himself.

'Ho! Young tree,' he cried, 'for days I have seen none of your tribe. How did you come to be the only tree on this empty plain?' Just then a breeze swept up the slope and rustled the sapling's leaves.

'Aha!' cried the boy. 'You talk, and I know what you say! Once you were a tiny seed — a papoose wrapped in white down. Your cradleboard swung from a twig. Then a strong Summer Wind came by. He lifted you from your mother's arms and brought you here. You see,' laughed the boy, 'I understand tree-talk! And I think he was a wise Wind. He planted your seed in this mud among sharp-edged rocks, where buffalo do not like to walk. But soon now they will reach over the rocks to scratch themselves against your branches. I'll make a stockade to protect you!' And the boy piled rocks higher around the lone sapling.

2. THE PEOPLE WHO WALKED

THE boy paused in his work beside the young sapling to watch his uncle on the butte. The scout waved a deerskin. It soared in wide sweeps, and danced in jerks. It signaled that buffalo were near, and might soon return to drink at the pond. A band of Kansas hunters saw the signals and walked toward the hill. But they were so far away that the boy saw only thin dots moving along the ancient trail. For another hour he piled stones around the young tree, chanting 'Ha! I am making you an island, an island of sharp rocks. Here you will be safe from the heavy hoofs when we hunt the Buffalo!'

Buffalo hunting on open plains was difficult for these Kansas Indians. When a few beasts in a herd were killed, the rest often stampeded for many miles without stopping. The Indians could not run after them, and as yet they had no horses. So hunts were planned to get a great many buffalo all at once. The hill of the twin buttes was known as a perfect place for such a hunting ground.

The boy paused again in his work. Now he could tell which dots on the trail were children and which were dogs. Each dog hauled a travois — poles spread out like the letter A, the wide ends dragging. These thirsty animals dashed forward when they smelled pond-water. The boy laughed to see bundles and lazy youngsters rolling off the racing, bouncing travois.

Women soon pitched buffalo-hide teepees near the pond. Children gathered buffalo-chips — sun-dried droppings of waste grass, the fuel for fires on the plains. A girl approached the young tree with a stone axe.

'No you don't!' said the boy quietly, stepping forward. 'If you need a stick to fix a travois, cut the end off an old teepee pole, but leave this sapling! Some day it will be a great tree to shade our people when we come again to this hill.'

SEVEN-BUFFALO-SKIN PATTERN, AND TEEPEE....Before Plains Indians got horses, most of them lived in earth-covered pole houses called "earth-lodges." Teepees, small and light enough to be hauled by dogs, were used mainly for hunting trips far from home.

PARFLECHE
(par-flesh)

TRAVOIS
(pronounced trav-wah)

EARTH-LODGES IN A VILLAGE

3. ARROWS AND SPEARS

'Ho!' called the scout from the butte top one morning. 'Far off, buffalo coming!'

At this news the Indian camp went wild. Children caught dogs and rolled bundles. Men dashed fires with water. Women flew at the teepees, which tumbled down like flapping birds. Everything seemed to be confusion. But in ten minutes women, children and dogs streaked down the east slope with all their possessions and vanished into a gully. Nothing remained of the camp but scattered ashes. Fifty men and some boys hugged the buttes so closely and lay so flat in the grass that only a flying hawk could see them.

The thirsty buffalo had seen nothing. They trotted up the west side of the hill, unable to scent danger against the wind. The sharp rocks fencing the young sapling split the herd, which rushed past to splash knee-deep in water. Pond and hilltop were hidden under a moving brown blanket of beasts; all but the island of rocks, where the little cottonwood tree stood bravely.

Arrows rained suddenly from the butte tops, hissed upward from the grassy slopes. Yearlings, cows and young bulls began falling at the edge of the herd. Those at the center did not know what was happening. They struggled with one another for a place to drink. A last shower of arrows killed many of those in the pond. This alarmed the whole herd and the animals wheeled and ran madly.

The hunters threw their spears at buffalo streaming below them. A river of buffalo rushed downhill like a muddy-brown flood. With a thunder of pounding hoofs they were gone, stampeding across the plain. But out of a thousand, nearly two hundred lay dead along the grassy slopes, and on the hilltop around the young tree.

4. THE FEASTING ON THE HILL

The Indians had walked many miles for this meat. Now there was plenty to take home to their village, far east in wooded country. Women and children danced for joy. Stern warriors cracked their faces in wide grins. Each hunter had emptied his quiver of twenty arrows, shooting so fast his fingers were numbed by the bowstring. The dead buffalo bristled like porcupines with those flint-pointed shafts Each boy told the next, time and again, just how he had done it.

Now came the women, with stone knives for the skinning. There was noisy feasting. All this fresh meat was too heavy for dogs to haul, and would quickly spoil on a journey. But dried meat weighed much less, and would keep for months. So strips of buffalo meat were hung from racks and ropes to dry a few days in the sun.

The boy walked to the young cottonwood and said, 'I think you brought my people this good luck. They hunted here before you came, but never killed so many. Here is a trophy that my arrows captured!' And he laid the black tail of a buffalo over a limb.

When the Indians started homeward, all extra travois were loaded. Even the children carried packs, and helped panting dogs to drag their loads. The most dignified warriors bent their backs under heavy burdens.

Wolves, coyotes, bears and foxes feasted when the Indians left. By day the sky was black with vultures, wheeling and dropping down. Crows and ravens squabbled over scraps. Magpies pecked at the buffalo tail until it fell from the tree. Birds and animals left only bones to bleach in the sun. And soon other buffalo came to the pond, not knowing or caring what had happened on the hill of the young cottonwood.

COYOTES and a WOLF

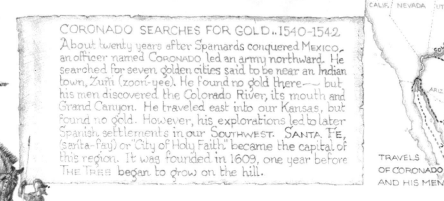

CORONADO SEARCHES FOR GOLD..1540-1542
About twenty years after Spaniards conquered Mexico,
an officer named CORONADO led an army northward. He
searched for seven golden cities said to be near an Indian
town, Zuñi (zoon-yee). He found no gold there—— but
his men discovered the Colorado River, its mouth and
Grand Canyon. He traveled east into our Kansas, but
found no gold. However, his explorations led to later
Spanish settlements in our SOUTHWEST. SANTA FE,
(santa-fay) or "City of Holy Faith" became the capital of
this region. It was founded in 1609, one year before
THE TREE began to grow on the hill.

TRAVELS
OF CORONADO
AND HIS MEN

5. A NEW ANIMAL ON THE PLAINS

THE cottonwood grew rapidly in its wet earth. But buffalo bulls fought near it, knocking down the boy's stockade. They ripped off its leaves, broke its branches and twisted its trunk. When the boy saw it again, he gasped 'so! My rocks did save your life, but could not keep you from being crippled. How you have changed in three summers! Now you look like a person! Yes, you are like a young girl bending forward, sign-talking. One bent arm says "come to me!" And the other says "now go that way, toward the setting sun, and take me with you!" But how could I carry a tree away from here? You must stay upon this hill!'

The tree was changing and so was life upon the Great Plains. Spaniards from Mexico had settled a region beyond the plains called 'New' Mexico, with its capital named 'Santa Fe.' Some Spanish horses had run away, becoming wild mustangs. At first, the Indians had been frightened by the horses, but not for long. They soon learned to ride like Spaniards.

This riding idea spread like wildfire. Tribes caught mustangs, or raided Spanish settlements for horses, or stole from one another. Pony-raiding started a new style of warfare. The people who had walked now rode everywhere, hunted buffalo on horseback and fought galloping games of war across the plains.

When the cottonwood tree was twenty feet tall, mounted Indians, with horses hauling large travois, camped at the pond. A young brave rode to the tree and hung a painted shield of buffalo-hide on a limb.

'A present, O Tree-Person,' he said. 'My first shield. Ever since saving your life I have had good luck, good medicine. In those days I walked. Now, see — I ride a horse!'

6. THE BEARER OF MESSAGES

ONE day a Sioux chief yanked the shield from its limb. 'Bah! Some dog of the Kansas thinks he owns these plains!' he grunted, hanging it lower on the trunk. 'But the tree!' said another warrior. 'It looks like a witch! Perhaps it's a magic tree!' At this the leader snorted. 'Then let it tell the Kansas what Dakota raiders think of them!' And ten flint-pointed arrows pinned the rawhide disc to the trunk as the laughing war party galloped past and away.

Winter winds tore the feathers from the shafts, and rain washed the paint off the shield. Then a Spanish priest came riding alone to the hill. His eyes were filled with a strange light when he saw the tree. Next morning he wrote in ink on the stained hide:

'18 August, 1623 — One Padre camped here, beneath this tree in the shape of a Sorrowing Madonna. From New Mexico's settlements he came eastward to comfort the heathen. If he returns not, know that his eyes have beheld an endless plain — a vast and beautiful land, fresh from the hand of Our Holy Father.'

Passing Indians puzzled over these strange marks, like dainty bird-tracks across the old shield. When years of rain had erased the tracks, Spanish soldiers spurred up the hill. One ripped the hide from its broken arrow-shafts and scorched big letters across its blank surface with hot irons:

'8 June, 1631 — 50 Spaniards from Santa Fe stopped by this Demon Tree in this cursed country! For horse stealing from our villages, 97 Indians we killed! May all Red Devils tremble! Long live the Sword!'

With a broken dagger blade driven deep he pinned the shield again to the trunk. Bitter winds tore it loose. But the stone arrow-points and the rusty sliver of steel had vanished under the growing wood of the tree that was a Witch, a Madonna or a Demon.

TREE RINGS MAKE CALENDARS

Sap, the lifeblood of a tree, flows through soft layers of fibers beneath the rough outer bark. Each year a new layer grows. Older ones harden into wood. When a tree is sawed lengthwise, the layers and their fibers show as "GRAIN" in lumber. When a tree is cut across, the layers show as "RINGS" — one for each year of life.
If the Cottonwood Tree had been cut when 25 years old, its rings would have looked like this.

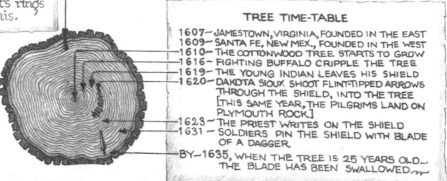

TREE TIME-TABLE

1607 — JAMESTOWN, VIRGINIA, FOUNDED IN THE EAST
1609 — SANTA FE, NEW MEX., FOUNDED IN THE WEST
1610 — THE COTTONWOOD TREE STARTS TO GROW
1616 — FIGHTING BUFFALO CRIPPLE THE TREE
1619 — THE YOUNG INDIAN LEAVES HIS SHIELD
1620 — DAKOTA SIOUX SHOOT FLINT-TIPPED ARROWS
THROUGH THE SHIELD, INTO THE TREE
[THIS SAME YEAR, THE PILGRIMS LAND ON
PLYMOUTH ROCK]
1623 — THE PRIEST WRITES ON THE SHIELD
1631 — SOLDIERS PIN THE SHIELD WITH BLADE
OF A DAGGER
BY ~1635, WHEN THE TREE IS 25 YEARS OLD —
THE BLADE HAS BEEN SWALLOWED

BALD
EAGLE

PRONG-HORNED
ANTELOPE

7. THE TALKING–TREE

WHATEVER the big cottonwood might be, animals and birds knew it only as a friend. Buffalo rubbed their sides against its trunk. Deer and antelope sought its cool shade. Prairie-hawks sat primly on its twig-tips; eagles swooped down to perch on its outstretched limb; and songsters speckled its great green crown with their nests.

Yet Indians wondered whether it was a good or an evil thing. In winter, stark and bare upon the lonely hill, it moaned in the bitter winds among its branches. On still nights, coyotes seemed to mourn for its moon-shadow, like a woman's ghost frozen on the snow. Even in summer, blanketed in leaves, it was a woman; listening, beckoning, pointing, and begging to be taken on the trail toward the setting sun. With every breeze it begged, chattering in its leaves. Was it not a Talking-Tree — a Medicine-Tree who knew and repeated any secret?

The Indians remembered an old shield on its trunk, seen three lifetimes ago. At first it had been scratched with bird tracks, sparrow-size. Later the marks grew big as an eagle's trail — scorched perhaps by the Thunderbird, Chief of Lightning! If it *was* a Medicine-Tree, then it could hear any war-plans made on the hill, tell them to the birds and thus warn the enemy!

At last a man from an eastern tribe stepped forward to end discussion. 'My Father saved this tree from the Buffalo-People,' he said. 'To it he gave his first shield. It is a Peace-Medicine-Tree, a shield against evil. No war should come near it. See, I give it a Peace-Offering!' And he tied a feathered pipe to a drooping branch.

Thus, across the plains, the Hill-Of-The-Talking-Tree became known as an island of peace set in the seas of war.

8. THE THUNDERBIRD SPEAKS

THE Talking-Tree was considered only a foolish myth by the Comanches, a northern tribe now roaming the Great Plains. Hard riders, hard fighters, they raided even New Mexican ranches whenever they wished.

A Comanche war party surprised two Pawnee braves, chasing them eastward day after day. The Pawnees reached the Hill-Of-Peace in a driving rain, pausing under the cottonwood to make the signs of 'Medicine-Tree.' Their enemies, coming within bowshot, only screamed their scorn and lashed their ponies faster.

The Comanches had arrows with points of Spanish iron. They yanked their bows from waterproof coverings, and began shooting at full gallop. Iron-tipped shafts tore through the rain and rattled, quivering, into the cottonwood trunk above the Pawnees.

Then it was true that Comanches had no respect for this sacred tree! The Pawnees kicked their tired ponies' ribs, speeding away. When they looked back the pursuers had topped the hill, were under the tree, still racing. But at that instant the world went blank in a flash of blinding white light.

When the Pawnees could look again, they saw only dark forms scattered between the buttes. Nothing moved on the hill but the mists of rain, and wisps of smoke from the tree. They dragged the bodies of their enemies far from the hill. Rain put out the fire that the lightning bolt had kindled. The tree was unharmed except for a jagged scar down the trunk like the mark of a giant claw.

To Indians, this accident was proof that the Thunderbird had spoken. From then on all tribes agreed that no war should ever come to the Hill-Of-Peace. And after that, even passing Comanches tied offerings to the twigs of the Talking-Tree.

Indians believed that a mythical THUNDERBIRD spirit ruled the skies. His beating wings made thunder. Lightning was the flashing of his eyes, the strike of his talons.

THE FRENCH IN AMERICA

Frenchmen carried on a great fur trade with Indians. Their Forts, on main canoe portages between water routes, held Canada, the Great Lakes and Mississippi Valley for France. After the French and Indian War, (1754-63), Britain held Canada and all French land (except New Orleans) westward to the Mississippi. Land west of the Mississippi, Louisiana Territory, was still French. So Frenchmen (probably never more than a few hundred in an entire century) crossed the plains, scattered in pairs through the lonely Rockies to trap, and traded with their neighbors to the south, the Spaniards.

9. TRAPPERS CROSS THE PLAINS

WITH passing years the tree grew larger, until birds nested in its branches seventy feet above the pond. Owls lived in a hollow where the lightning had burned. Growing wood long since had swallowed the Comanche arrowpoints of iron. The Medicine-Tree was now a century old.

While Spaniards had been settling New Mexico, Frenchmen had come to eastern Canada. They paddled canoes up the St. Lawrence, through the Great Lakes and down the Mississippi River to the Gulf. Towns sprang up around their forts where Indians bartered furs for blankets and brass kettles. A few French trappers rode west across the plains. Packhorses carried their steel traps, as well as cloth, small mirrors and beads, tickets of safe travel among Spaniards and Indians.

The Spaniards liked the French. Indians liked the presents. And so, for the next hundred years, small bands of trappers roamed the Rocky Mountains, where the mountain streams fairly boiled with beaver. At Taos and Santa Fe, in New Mexico, Frenchmen sold beaver pelts for Spanish silver and gold. Some trappers settled down in these sunny towns. Others returned across the plains to St. Louis and New Orleans, with tales of riches and adventure.

A few Americans drifted west to the Rockies, following the French — hunters and trappers who liked plenty of elbow room. Crossing the plains, the first of these Mountain Men camped on the hill with friendly Pawnees, and asked a chief, 'What's all the fooferaw danglin' from this twisted tree? Why all the fuss and feathers?'

'Peace offerings to this Tree-Of-Peace,' explained the chief, and told its story. And thus, from St. Louis to Santa Fe, Mountain Men retold the tale until the cottonwood was over two centuries old.

CANADA

LAKE SETTLEMENTS

QUEBEC

MONTREAL

ENGLISH SETTLEMENTS

THE ROCKIES, LAND OF TRAPPERS, MOUNTAIN MEN TERRITORY OF LOUISIANA

TREE

ST. LOUIS

FRENCH RIVER

TAOS
SANTA FE

SPANISH SETTLEMENTS

EL PASO

NEW ORLEANS

Gulf of Mexico

ON THE MAP

■ = FR. FORTS
O = TOWNS
P. = PORTAGE FOR CANOES
TRAILS====

Most beaver fur made felt for "Beaver Hats." "Fooferaw" was frontier lingo for "fancy fixings." This hat has fooferaw.

TAOS PUEBLO (pronounced TOWSE PWEB-LOW) was for years a favorite meeting and trading place of the Southwest. Here were held "Trappers' Fairs," and everyone came~French and American trappers, or "Mountain Men," Spaniards, and Indians of many tribes.

AMERICA BUYS SOME LAND

After the French and Indian War (1754-63), the American Colonies separated from England (Revolutionary War, 1775-83). Meanwhile, the territory of Louisiana west of the Mississippi was given by French treaty to Spain, and later taken back again. In 1803 the United States bought Louisiana from Napoleon, Emperor of France. This doubled the size of America, which soon reached from the Atlantic to the Pacific. Thus the SANTA FE TRAIL was to run across American plains. But the end of it, and Santa Fe itself, still belonged to the King of Spain.

10. WHEELS TURN ON THE SANTA FE TRAIL

WHEN Mountain Men returned to the Mississippi River towns people listened to the tales of their adventures.

'Those Spaniards at Santa Fe,' reported one veteran, 'have more gold and silver than a dog's got fleas, but no place to spend it. All their fancy store-things come clear from Old Mexico, over mountain trails bad enough to break a snake's back. The goods get busted, arrive months late, and cost ten times their worth.

'For a hundred years, off and on, Frenchmen have peddled do-dads to New Mexico for plenty of profit. No big mountains bar their way across the plains, but they use only packhorses. Now, *wagons* could roll west to Santa Fe like buckshot across a cabin floor! Americans could sell wagon loads of goods cheaper than Spanish merchants from Mexico, and still get plenty rich!'

Such talk set men to thinking. Soon steamboats with New England cargoes plowed the Mississippi to St. Louis. Later they chugged farther west up the Missouri River, unloading along the shores. Store-houses sprang up to shelter the goods. Towns sprang up around the storehouses. Then covered wagons, packed with these cargoes, rolled westward on the Trail to Santa Fe. . . .

When the first wagons neared the tree in the Trail, an Indian boy called from a butte, 'Father, I see great white animals crawling!'

'They are not animals, though animals pull them,' said the man below. 'They are huge cloth-covered boxes, and they roll on spinning shields. In a dream-vision I saw others like them, stopping on this hill. When they went away, a strange thing happened. The Medicine-Tree was leading them along the ancient buffalo trail.'

THE TRAIL OF GOODS FROM MEXICO

Santa Fe   RATON HILL   THE TRAIL FROM "THE STATES"

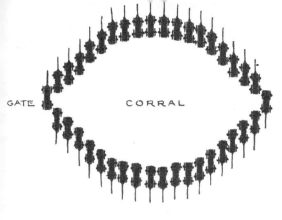

TWO TYPES OF WAGON CAMPS

The circle stockade made a fort and a corral. Men cooked, slept and played games outside the big circle after the daily fifteen miles. Wagons traveled four abreast. With twelve animals hauling each, forty wagons used about five hundred, plus eight hundred spares. Such trains had a hundred men with three hundred riding horses. The camps were busy places!

GATE CORRAL

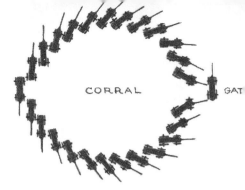

CORRAL GAT

11. JED AND BUCK

Buck Smith, son of a Mountain Man, had grown up in Missouri forests. From his dead father he inherited Old Martha (a Kentucky flintlock rifle), a sound knowledge of woodcraft, and many tales of the plains and mountains. Jed Simpson, from an Ohio farm, was not a woodsman like Buck. But he could build almost anything in wood or iron, and knew more about horses, oxen and wagons than most men. These two young fellows had joined a caravan for their first (and almost their last) trip on the Santa Fe Trail.

Their wagon train had camped at Cow Creek, miles east of the tree in the Trail. Fresh meat was needed, so twenty hunters, Jed and Buck included, rode toward a huge buffalo herd. They approached through deep ravines, unseen by the buffalo. When they spurred their horses to the open plain, the shaggy animals promptly stampeded.

In the confusion Jed Simpson found himself alone, surrounded by ten thousand madly running beasts. His pony galloped beside a fat buffalo. Jed's rifle dropped it beneath thundering hoofs. While Jed was reloading at breakneck speed, a thong broke and his powder horn was lost. His shooting was over. He could only hang on, hoping his racing mount would not stumble and fall. After what seemed hours, he worked his horse toward the edge of the charging herd. The last buffalo streamed past him, the thunder of hoofs died to a murmur, the dust rolled away.

Jed dismounted from his weary pony. His mind still rocked with bounding bodies, and his ears roared. Wondering where he was and where the caravan might be, he saw a distant horseman. Was it an Indian? Jed grasped his rifle — then realized that it was useless. Except for his heavy hunting knife, he was unarmed.

FLINTLOCKS

FLINT WRAPPED IN BUCKSKIN TO CUSHION THE BLOW

THE STEEL

HAMMER

THIS FIRING PART IS THE "LOCK."

BARREL

"OLD MARTHA", BUCK'S RIFLE

GUNPOWDER "PRIMES" THE PAN

PATCH BOX

CURLY-MAPLE STOCK

Flintlocks are loaded from muzzle. A small spoonful of gunpowder is sifted in, followed by ball (lead bullet), wrapped in a tiny square of greased cloth or buckskin — the "patch", rammed down with ramrod. "Pan" is "primed." Hammer strikes a few sparks with "flint" on "steel" — fire from priming goes through a hole in barrel, and gun "fires."

COMBINED POWDER HORN AND BULLET POUCH.

TRIGGER-GUARD

TRIGGER

The bow-case protected bow and string
(twisted sinew fibers from along a deer's
backbone).
The quiver's opening was often lined
with fur. This kept the feathered shafts
from slipping out, and prevented noisy
rattling.

12. THE RACE FOR LIFE

JED was relieved when the horseman turned out to be Buck Smith.

'What you aimin' to do — chase them woolly cows plumb to Santy Fee?' exploded Buck, reining in his sweaty mount.

'Shot one, then lost my powder horn,' explained Jed lamely.

'Bet I chased you ten miles,' Buck grunted. 'What's that over yonder? Looks like the rest of our party gallopin' this way. Nope, by gum, it's *Injuns!* Here, take my powder horn an' load as you ride! But if you drop *that* horn, I'll scalp you my own self!'

The two raced west at top speed. Jed stood in his stirrups, ramming powder and ball down his rifle barrel.

'Them Arapaho is gainin' on us!' howled Buck over his shoulder. 'Ride fer that hill ahead — two buttes an' a tree! We'll fight 'em from that cover, *if* we *git* there!'

In five more minutes, the two reached the foot of the hill. The Indians lashed their horses. They made frantic efforts to come within bowshot, but their arrows zipped to earth short of their mark.

'Made it!' gasped Buck, leaping from his saddle. 'Skin yourself off that nag an' up one rockpile — I'll take the other! Lie flat as a turtle on top of that butte, an' aim true when you shoot!'

'But the Injuns!' yelled Jed. 'They've stopped! Look at 'em!'

'*What?*' cried Buck. 'Well, I'm a buzzard's uncle! If they ain't laughin' an' wavin' goodby! Like we was playin' a game, an' had reached a goal or somethin'! HEY! You snake-eyed paint-faces, come on an' fight like men! We'll carve out your gizzards! We'll —'

'Aw, don't urge 'em so much,' panted Jed, leaning against the tree. 'If they feel like leavin', don't press 'em to stay. As fer myself, I'm mighty happy with jest the two of us here!'

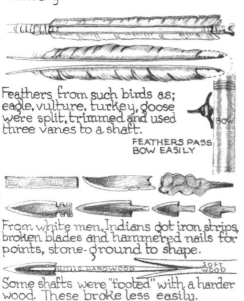

INDIAN ARROWS

POINT   SHAFT   FEATHERING   NOCK

Stone points of chert, quartz, obsidian
(black volcanic glass) had many shapes.
The split end of the shaft straddled a
point. Wet sinew binding shrank tight
when dry.

Feathers from such birds as;
eagle, vulture, turkey, goose
were split, trimmed and used
three vanes to a shaft.

FEATHERS PASS
BOW EASILY

From white men, Indians got iron strips,
broken blades and hammered nails for
points, stone-ground to shape.

Some shafts were "footed" with a harder
wood. These broke less easily.

FOOTED SHAFT

13. POST OFFICE TREE

THE Indians rode out of sight, leaving two puzzled youths behind.

'Look!' cried Jed. 'Feathers an' ribbons danglin' up there! I swan! This old tree's wavin' its arms, ready to speak a piece!'

Buck squinted up, down and all about. 'A pond, two buttes, a tree like an old squaw —' he muttered slowly. 'Yup! This is *her!* Jed, you ever hear of a Talkin'-Tree? Of course not. Well, Injuns told my paw, a Mountain Man, what they wouldn't tell other whites. This here's a Medicine-Tree ——' and Buck talked while the sun sank, and stars shimmered like tiny candle flames among the matted twigs.

Next afternoon the wagons came rolling like white-sailed ships on a grassy sea, and camped around the pond. The others were surprised to find the two young men alive. That morning, painted warriors had attacked the train at Cow Creek. But the circle of wagons (with all livestock safe inside it) was too strong a stockade, and they had ridden away.

When the two told their story, the caravan captain was surprised. 'Never did know why Injuns hung do-dads on these limbs,' he said. 'Nor why they never ambushed us from these rocks. Us wagon men nowadays know your "Medicine-Tree" as plain "Old Post Office." This hollow, where lightning burned once, is where we post letters for anybody, goin' in the right direction, to carry to civilization.'

That evening Jed and Buck watched firelight flicker up the trunk.

'Think of it!' said Jed softly, staring upward. 'We've been saved by this old cottonwood! I'll never forget that, long as I live!'

'Well, don't feel too solemn about it,' yawned Buck from his blankets. 'Plenty men have died on trees afore now, an' under 'em. It's only fair fer some tree to do somebody some good fer a change!'

SALINE RIVER
SOLOMON R.
SMOKY HILL R.
KANSAS A TERRITORY—1854
KANSAS A STATE ——1861
TOPEKA
KANSAS RIVER
KANSAS CITY 1839
A treaty with Osages (1825) for right-of-way of the TRAIL, gave its name to COUNCIL GROVE
Baldwin City
Olathe
Burlingame
THE TRAIL
NEOSHO RIVER
LOST SPRINGS
DIAMOND SPRINGS
COTTONWOOD CREEK
TREE

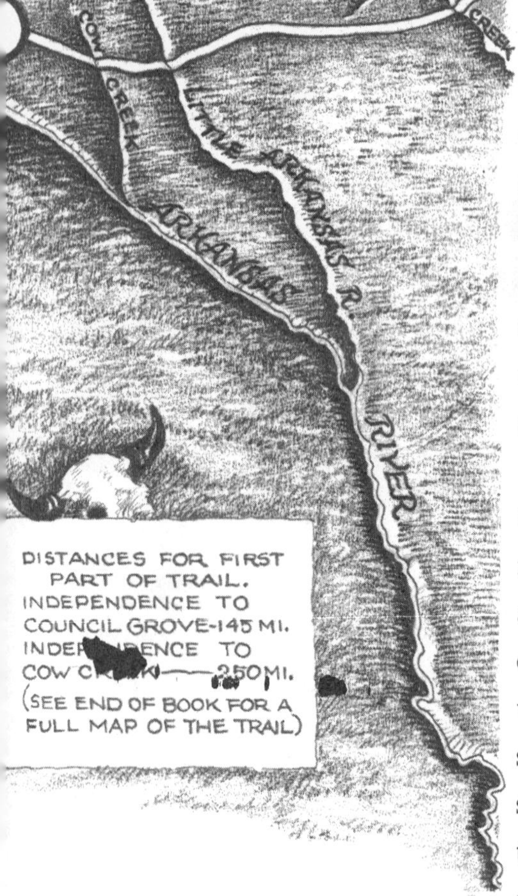
COW CREEK
LITTLE ARKANSAS R.
ARKANSAS RIVER
DISTANCES FOR FIRST PART OF TRAIL.
INDEPENDENCE TO COUNCIL GROVE-145 MI.
(SEE END OF BOOK FOR A FULL MAP OF THE TRAIL)

14. COTTONWOODS DON'T LIVE FOREVER

In the years following, Jed Simpson became known as the best wagon-master on the Santa Fe Trail. Each Spring, when the prairie grass was tall enough for horses and oxen to eat, small groups of covered wagons left the town of Independence on the Missouri. They collected about one hundred fifty miles farther west, in a woodland called Council Grove. Here Jed was usually chosen as captain of the combined wagon train for the trip. And Buck Smith was Chief Scout and head of the guards.

It was always a high spot of the journey after Council Grove when the train neared the tree in the Trail. Jed and Buck would ride ahead, remembering the wild ride they once had made. Before the wagons arrived they would examine Old Post Office to see how it had weathered the icy gales of the winter before. When Buck wasn't looking, Jed would give the gnarled trunk a friendly pat. 'Thanks again,' he would say, 'for saving us.' And he always mailed a letter in the hollow for some eastbound person to carry back to Independence, telling the trader for whom he worked how the trip was going. He also included a few words from Buck, who could not write.

Buck was forever finding the tree worse off than the year before. He would count the dead branches. Each season there were more. Jed kept saying that the tree would pull through many another year, but at this Buck usually exploded.

'After all,' he would say, 'it's only cottonwood, an' cottonwoods don't live forever. They ain't even got the life-span of a basswood. This here tree is old because it's always had a water supply from the spring pond. She's already sixty-some years overdue to die. An' she's dyin' from the top down, sure as shootin'!' But, though he knew the truth, Jed would not give in.

15. THE OLD TREE DIES

ONE year, Spring came quickly to the white-robed plains. Snow melted from the rusty grass, rain fell, and the earth was alive with water. But, though moisture soaked the old tree's roots, new sap did not rise again in that ancient bark.

And so the tree was dead. It had been a companion to bird, beast and man. Now it stood bare upon the windswept hill — no longer a living thing, but a piece of wood. Yet to the buffalo who rubbed against its trunk, it did not seem changed. Birds still flocked among its leafless branches. Its top limb still pointed out the Trail, as if to say — 'There it lies. Yonder lies the Trail to golden deserts and the high, far hills! Seasons and centuries have passed me by while I stood rooted to the earth. But westward lie shining mountains against a brighter sky. Go that way. . . . Go that way. . . .'

When the new grass was tall enough for forage, Jed's wagons came rumbling along the Trail. The two friends rode toward the hill.

'By gum,' said Buck, gazing carefully ahead, 'she's dead! Old Post Office has passed to the Happy Huntin' Grounds!'

'You're crazy,' replied Jed, squinting hard. 'I see leaves.'

'Playin' cards by moonlight has plumb ruined your eyesight,' snorted Buck. 'Either that or you jest can't face the truth. I'll lay you ten to two they ain't no green feathers on that timber!'

'I'll take the bet!' growled Jed. 'But remember — one leaf, one little green bud even, an' she's still alive!'

That evening by the campfire Jed slowly printed a note. And, when next morning's sun arose on the disappearing wagons, a sunbeam crept into the old hollow, lighting this message:

JUNE-11-1834-NOTICE TO ANY WAGON DRIVER—MOUNTAIN MAN—OR OTHER ANIMAL WHICH CAN READ THIS LETTER PLEASE TAKE IT TO CHRIS JOHNSON, TRADER, AT INDEPENDENCE AND I THANK YOU KINDLY.

DEAR MR. JOHNSON: CAMPED THIS DATE AT POST OFFICE TREE AFTER GOOD TRIP 20 DAYS OUT. THIS SEASON LOOKS GOOD. NO BAD STORMS COMING THIS YEAR. ALL MEN AND ANIMALS WELL, BUT——

THE OLD TREE IS DEADER THAN A WHEEL SPOKE. HOPING YOU THE SAME I BEG TO REMAIN YOURS TRULY JED X. SIMPSON. P.S. BUCK SAYS SO TOO.

16. A KANSAS TWISTER

JED had written 'no bad storms coming this year.' None struck the caravan on the way to Santa Fe. Halfway back, however, it rained rivers, and the wagons bogged down in mud. When a playful tornado spun like a top across the plain, the men had time to save most of their animals by chasing them into a ravine. But five of the best wagons vanished in that wild blast. Jed said afterwards 'it give us all a mighty funny feelin' to see them big prairie schooners flyin' off like birds.' Years later, Indians found wagon-parts scattered across the trackless plain. Their Medicine Men decided these things had dropped from the sky. And for once they were right.

A sorry-looking train crawled back to the hill. But no tree now stood in the Trail. The tornado had split its trunk and thrown it down.

'By gum!' said Buck, scratching his bearded chin on the end of his ramrod. 'This *is* the end of her! Now she sure *has* gone to the Happy Huntin' Grounds. She ain't good for nothin' no more.'

'Some of her's good for somethin' yet!' cried Jed. 'Her job ain't finished. I need timber for a new ox yoke!'

'Out of *cottonwood*?' snorted Buck. 'Anybody knows it rots out sudden. Why, the wood busts if you give it a swift look even! An' yet you'll use this here pie crust fer an *OX YOKE*? You're loco, sure!'

'That Kansas twister stole all my spare yokes, an' I need one bad,' explained Jed. 'An' I suppose you'll ride a hundred miles east to Council Grove an' fetch me back a stick of good basswood or oak? I thought not. So I'll jest use what the good Lord provided, an' be thankful!'

There are many types of
yokes. This odd eight-foot
yoke hauls timber. One
end of a log chained to it
is off the ground; other end
drags. Oxen have plenty
of room for working.

Each yo[ke]
its chai[n]
hook a[t]

17. THE PAST COMES TO LIGHT

So, WHILE the animals grazed and the men hunted fresh meat, Jed Simpson made a cottonwood ox yoke. He had hacked out many a good yoke in a few hours, but this took two days and a night. There were several reasons for this, which he came upon after cutting a seasoned length. He had begun hewing it down when his axe struck something hard. The blade was badly nicked.

'What in blazes!' roared Jed, carefully chopping around that place. When Buck rode in with an antelope behind his saddle, he found Jed quite excited.

'Look!' Jed cried, pointing to the chunk. 'An entire curio shop! Two stone arrowheads there. (That's ancient history, before Injuns got iron.) Here's a sliver of steel (an' if it ain't part of a Spanish dagger then I'm a chipmunk)! Where these tree rings are younger, three arrowpoints of iron. (Injuns are now tradin' with the whites.) An' to finish off, this dark bulge is a lead ball from a French trapper's old-time smoothbore (a hundred years old, easy). Think of it, Buck! Right before our eyes, ancient history comin' to light — things the old tree has swallowed in her past!'

'Even so,' grinned Buck, bowing low. 'But there's somethin' lackin'. Why not bring your collection up to date?' And, still bent over, he swung his rifle under his arm and pulled the trigger. Jed leaped backward, holding both ears and coughing in the cloud of smoke streaming from the rifle barrel.

'There!' chuckled Buck. 'Now your woodpile carries a bullet of today, along with the other curios. As neat a nubbin of lead as Old Martha, Queen of Kentucky Rifles, ever tossed out!'

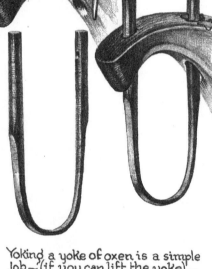

Yoking a yoke of oxen is a simple
job — (if you can lift the yoke)...
Drive the oxen to the yoke; make
them stand together; swing the
heavy timber across the necks;
slip the hickory ox-bows up and
set the pegs, and the patient ox-
en are all yoked up.
You drive oxen with your lungs.
A driver or "Bull-whacker" walks
(on the Trail, they always walked)
beside the left or "near" ox, next
the wagon. "G'lang" starts them
(the old-time Bull-whackers had
words in six languages for this),
"Gee" steers them right, "Haw" to
the left, "Whoa" for a stop, and
"Back" for reverse.
If the right-hand (or "off") ox takes
fright and both run away, there
is nothing you can do but led it
along after them, yelling!!!

Yoke-ring of "wheel-oxen" fits
over tongue, hook fastens to
bolt. From here on, as many
yoke as are needed are
"hooked up."

TONGUE

HEAD-BOARD
AND BELL-BAR

(SAME)
PIECE

TRAPPER'S BULLET
FROM SMOOTH-
BORE (GUN
WITH NO
RIFLING IN
BARREL)

TWO IRON ARROWHEADS

OLD MARTHA'S BULLET

ONE IRON
ARROW-
HEAD

TWO STONE ARROWHEADS   SPANISH DAGGER

HOW
SPLIT
TRE

18. THE OX YOKE

**HOW JED MADE
THE YOKE**

'You hot-headed hop-toad!' Jed sputtered. 'Why shoot this wood? Made a hole almost through it for nothin'. Bullet don't even show!'

'Peel this bulge on the other side,' said Buck calmly. 'It'll show.'

All this gave Jed an idea. He shaped the yoke carefully, so that all the curios could be seen. It would be a large yoke.

'That's hoss sense,' said Buck, really interested. 'Leave enough wood on her an' she *might* last to Independence.'

'She'll last,' grunted Jed. 'If you want to help instead of jest hinder, soak up that bull buffalo hide the men brought in.'

Most of that night Jed worked by firelight. His hunting knife and spoke-shave made soft, hissing sounds. Next morning Buck was astonished.

'By gum!' he said. 'Fanciest stick of timber ever I see. Fancy enough, even, for a Spaniard. But no matter how slick you carve her, she's bound to bust. Remember, she's cottonwood to the core!'

'Don't jabber!' ordered Jed. 'Shave the hair off that wet hide!'

When Jed had finished, all the wagon men stood around in wonder. He had covered the yoke with rawhide stretched tight and nailed. When it dried, the hide would shrink tighter. Besides this, an iron band and six bolts made certain that the cottonwood could never split. Each curio, including Buck's bullet, poked through its own slit in the buffalo skin and was circled with brass studs. The ox bows, seasoned hickory from an old yoke, were painted red on top. The crowning glory was a set of silver bells, which sang with any movement of the yoke.

'So that Spanish seen-yor-eeta at Santa Fe *did* give you them bells, after all!' chuckled Buck. 'But anyhow, this here is the slickest, prettiest yoke ever to start a run on the Trail!'

And all the men agreed, she sure-as-shootin' was!

SANTA FE TRAIL
1834

THE YOKE

19. THE YOKE GOES TO INDEPENDENCE

AND so the best part of the ancient cottonwood tree went traveling. No more was it rooted to one lonely spot while the world rolled past. It lay across the necks of two big oxen, Starbright and Bugle, leading the caravan. It swung with silver bells, and traveled with a tune.

At Independence, the head of the Trail, steamboats splashed up the muddy Missouri with new cargoes. Negroes carted bales and barrels to the stores. Those boxes of glassware, perfumes, cloth, food and hardware brought riches in the Santa Fe trade. And so merchants in silk hats bowed to silk-gowned ladies riding in polished carriages.

Frenchmen from Canada and New Orleans arrived by canoe. Blanketed Indians on spotted ponies wondered at the giant Smoke-Boats, always on fire, that never burned down. Americans from the civilized East laughed with amusement at this raw West. To Mountain Men bringing furs from the Rockies, this was civilization itself. Barber-shops, dancehalls and hotels did a brisk business.

Jed Simpson had counted the growth of tree rings on the cotton-wood when he made the yoke. Now under each curio he burned its date. Crowds gathered at the window of Chris Johnson's store, where Jed worked, to see the yoke. When Indians learned where it came from, they jabbered excitedly.

Winter blizzards howled down the icy river from the open plains, and the town slept. But when the ice went out and snow melted under warm winds, Buck Smith rode in with news. 'Buffalo herds grazing north again,' he cried. 'Grass is up!'

The stores buzzed like hives of bees. Loaded wagons left town to gather at Council Grove. Jed said goodby to Chris Johnson, and led his train away. And the yoke started westward to Santa Fe with Star-bright and Bugle, singing its silver tunes.

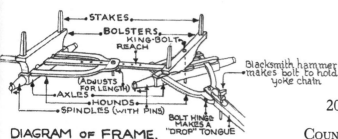

- STAKES.
- BOLSTERS.
- KING-BOLT.
- REACH

Blacksmith hammer makes bolt to hold yoke chain

(ADJUSTS FOR LENGTH)
- AXLES
- HOUNDS.
- SPINDLES (WITH PINS)

BOLT HINGE MAKES A "DROP" TONGUE

DIAGRAM OF FRAME,
CALLED **RUNNING-GEAR** (WHEELS OFF).

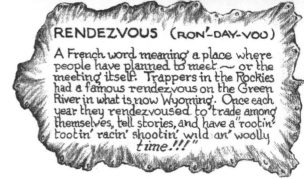

RIM

THE WHEEL
The HUB holds SPOKES which fit into several FELLIES, making the RIM. An iron TIRE holds all parts together.

THE WAGON-BOX sits on bolsters, held there by stakes. Wooden strips on outside, chains inside, strengthen walls.

HOOPS in brackets
TOOL-BOX.
BRAKE-LEVER (pulled by driver with rope or chain)
BRAKE.

Bucket with tar for wheel-greasing

THE COVER is an oblong of canvas with drawstrings at ends. When the strings are all tight and sides laced down, it makes a tent protecting the goods inside.

The wagon sketched here is Conestoga type. Types on the TRAIL changed as manufacturers of Pittsburgh, St. Louis, Independence and finally Kansas City redesigned them.

A loaded wagon weighed from 1½ to 3½ TONS and needed about six yoke of oxen or twelve mules to haul it across the Plains.

20. RENDEZVOUS AT COUNCIL GROVE

COUNCIL GROVE had the last stand of hardwood on the march westward. Here men made spare parts for their wagons from oak, walnut, maple and hickory. Axes rang, trees crashed, mauls thudded on wedges and logs split open. Hand-saws buzzed, planes and draw-shaves hissed through wood. And the ground was littered with golden curls 'like the floor of a Dutch barbershop,' as Buck said.

Here the men cleaned everything, even themselves. Splashing and laughter rolled along the shady creek. Curious fish swirled through soapy water and swam away in disgust. Crows and thrushes were puzzled when bushes suddenly bloomed with woolens hung to dry.

Small wagon trains came to Council Grove like streams to a river, joining together for better protection against hostile Indians. When a captain was elected to head this larger caravan, Jed Simpson was chosen as usual.

One June morning Jed rolled out of his blankets in the gray dawn to call his first order: 'Catch up! Catch up!' Immediately men raced through the dark to catch and harness their neighing horses, bawling oxen or braying mules. Yoke chains clanked, rings rattled. But soon, from woods and glades, drivers began calling 'All's set!' as their outfits were ready. At the last call, the captain yelled 'Stretch out!' and the wagons rumbled into place in the gray light. Jed standing on a wheel hub, counted forty-one. They were strung out in four rows of ten each, his own in front, like a fleet of sailing ships in a fog, awaiting a breeze.

And Jed X. Simpson supplied the breeze. He carefully smoothed his beard, cupped his hands to his mouth, took a deep breath and bellowed 'FALL–L–L–L *IN*!' like a bull roaring. Starbright and Bugle lunged against the cottonwood yoke. Men yelled. Whips cracked. And one hundred sixty-four wheels started turning toward Santa Fe.

Site of now-ruined Bent's Fort. Kit Carson once lived here. His house in Taos still stands.

(Pueblo)

(La Junta)

ArKANSAS RIVER

(Syracuse) (Garden City)

(Dodge City)

CIMARRON CROSSING

COLO. KANS.

THE TREE

(Great Bend)

(Hutchinson)

CH. FO. PA.

After the rains of 1834 this desert cut-off was plainly marked by wheel ruts. It later came to be the main route, but water had to be hauled in barrels over parts of this trail.

Dry Cimarron River

CIMARRON Route

KA. OKL.

Trinidad

RATON PASS

PURGATOIRE RIVER

Raton

COLO. N.M.

TAOS PUEBLO, 3 miles from TAOS, for years the end of THE TRAIL.

Springer

TAOS TRAIL

Wagon Mound

SANTA FE

Fort Union

PECOS RUINS

(Las Vegas)

CANADIAN R.

PECOS R.

21. RETURN TO THE HILL

Over a hundred miles stretched between Council Grove and the hill of the twin buttes. Wheel ruts of the Trail gouged the earth like plowed furrows. The wagons traveled four abreast so as to keep bunched together in case of attack, and at night were formed into a circle stockade.

'Injuns near-by, thick as Kansas sunflowers!' reported Buck. But, though armed guards kept alert, no war-whoops split the early dawns.

At last the hill camp was reached, and the wagons circled the pond. Jed and Buck sprawled on their blankets under the stars.

'Seems funny not to see her spreadin' above us, don't it?' said Jed. 'But if a tree could think, I'll bet she's mighty glad to be a yoke, swingin' along, tinklin' pretty. That tree was too held down. Always pointin' as if she wanted to follow us on the Trail. Now she can go beyond her hill, away out yonder — farther than she ever dreamed.

'Maybe it's that way with people, sort of. They git rooted down, too. Along comes disaster, or what looks like it, an' they feel lost. But maybe, if they only knew — all that's happened to 'em is that they've been freed. Freed to go farther than they ever thought. Maybe they's bells waitin' for them, too   Bells that will tinkle inside 'em some-where. . . .'

'Huh!' snorted Buck. 'Maybe you should be wonderin' why Injuns ain't after our hair, now that the tree ain't here to protect this hill. They're so near I can mighty nigh smell 'em, but they don't attack!'

'They won't attack,' replied Jed calmly. 'I explained plenty about the yoke to them Injuns back in Independence. They sent the word along. The tribes now think the Peace-Medicine lives on in the yoke. The old tree's spirit is still savin' us from harm.'

Buffalo bulls often gouged the earth with their horns and rolled in the dust. This wild play made saucer-shaped BUFFALO WALLOWS, used year after year.
Buffalo birds (now called "cow blackbirds") followed the herds, eating ticks from the woolly backs.

22. HOW THE WHEELS ROLLED WESTWARD

AND so the yoke left its hill and traveled westward. The Trail hugged the flat banks of the Arkansas River, bordered by sandhills. The eastern half of Kansas had grass so tall a boy could be lost in it. But here grew gamma grass, no longer than a finger. Buffalo grazed everywhere upon it. Sometimes they covered the plains like a moth-eaten brown robe, and their criss-cross trails lay over the earth like a fishnet, leading through the sandhills and down to the Arkansas.

Dust from the caravan hid the Trail, the animals' legs, the turning wheels. The beasts seemed to swim in a golden mist, followed by lazy ships. But this travel was not as easy as it looked. Axles moaned. Ox-bows squealed in their sockets. There was a groaning of wood and iron as tons of weight moved slowly forward.

Horses and mules ran sweat like soapsuds, but the oxen were dry as boards. They could sweat only on the muzzle, and their noses gleamed like varnished leather. There was only one thought in these beasts' heads — to lift one heavy hoof ahead of the other. When they lagged, long whips cracked like pistol shots, up and down the train, and sweating drivers bellowed themselves hoarse in a swinging chant:

'Get *on*, you heaving hunks of rawhide! *Lift* those hoofs! *Where* were you born — in a *buck*et of cold mo*lasses*? G'*lang*, you Bud! G'*lang*, you Bill! Git *movin'* you *PETE*! I'll *roll* you in thunder an' *grease* your tails in lightnin' — an' *sizz*le you *pink* in the *skill*et of that thar *SUN*!'

But, where Jed walked beside the leading wagon, no whip ever struck Starbright or Bugle. They proudly led the train of rocking schooners to the tinkle of bells.

BENT'S FORT
The building has been
sketched after an
old print.

ADOBE (AH-DOH-BAY)

In the Southwest it means
a sun-dried mud brick, or
the mud plaster, or plain
mud.

23. AT BENT'S FORT

AT CIMARRON CROSSING Jed called a council of wagon drivers.

'Shall we cut south across waterless desert, or tackle Raton Hill by way of Bent's Fort?' he asked.

'Bent's Fort!' they answered. 'We don't hanker to die thirsty!'

Two hundred miles farther on they came to the Fort. It was not an army post (though sixty men were needed to run it and keep it supplied), but a trading post built by the famous Bent Brothers. Its adobe walls, four feet thick and almost two stories high, stood on a sage-brush plain like a lonely castle. Here the Santa Fe Trail crossed another running from Mexico north to Canada. Every western traveler stopped here at some time in his life. Teepees clustered outside the walls. Though tribes might be at war, they met here in peace to trade their furs for trinkets.

Heavy wooden gates creaked open to let the wagon men through. One of the Bents, wearing beaded buckskins, greeted Jed and Buck.

'So you made a safe journey again,' he said, smiling. 'This time I was dead sure you would. My scouts have told me all about the yoke. And I've invited a hundred braves to see that traveling piece of their old Medicine-Tree.'

The fort buildings faced inward on an open square, or patio, lined with porches. Here the Indians gathered in their finest costumes.

'Stew me fer a buffalo hump!' exclaimed Buck. 'The red people have sure turned out! Look, Jed! There's Sioux from Dakota country; Kiowas, Apaches and Comanches from down near Mexico; Pawnees an' Kansas; Crows an' Blackfeet from the north; Cheyennes an' Utes out of the Rockies; an' Pueblo Injuns from Taos an' the Rio Grande! Enough hate an' bitter tribal feelin's in this bunch to blow the Fort wide open. Yet they're pow-wowin' like brothers around the yoke. An' all over a chunk of worthless cottonwood!'

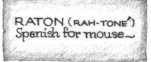
RATON (RAH-TONE')
Spanish for mouse

YUCCA
(YUK-KAH)

SAGE BUSH AND
PRAIRIE DOGS

PRICKLY- PEAR
CACTUS

CHOLLA (CHOY-YAH)
CACTUS

24. THE HILL THAT WAS CALLED A MOUSE

THE Fort's blacksmith shop clanged for days while men re-shod horses and oxen, and repaired wagons. Then the caravan turned south, because its western way was cut off by a blue wall — the Rocky Mountains.

Troubles lay ahead. In desert dotted with greasewood, sage, cactus and yucca, wagons turned over in ravines and were slowly re-loaded. Then a mountain blocked their way — a hill called 'Raton,' which is Spanish for 'mouse.'

While crossing this 'mouse,' men and animals almost died with effort. There was no way open but up, up, up. The snakelike Trail wiggled in sharp zig-zags. Struggling hoofs sent rocks crashing down on wagons below. Extra beasts were added to all teams. Starbright and Bugle led forty oxen hitched to Jed's schooner. But, even with twenty men straining at the wheel spokes, it moved upward only inches at a time. This was a cruel test for the cottonwood yoke, yet it did not break. At day's end, men and animals were exhausted. And still they must climb higher than Buck's rifle could shoot.

It was three full days before the last outfit rested atop Raton Hill, almost two miles above sea-level. Winds fresh from the snowy peaks sighed through great pines. New Mexico's deserts stretched southward below them, golden in the sun. Tangled ribbons of the Trail braided together and vanished in distance. Men tied wheels to stop their turning, roped tree trunks against them to drag as extra brakes. And the caravan slid and skidded on its dangerous journey down.

After such torture, the rest of the trip was a merry journey. They passed the ruins of Pecos Pueblo, which Coronado had visited almost three centuries before. They climbed easily through Glorietta Pass, and camped one night on a plateau smelling of pine and cedar. Below, like a meeting of fireflies, a cluster of tiny lights blinked dimly. There in the velvet darkness lay Santa Fe.

25. THE YOKE COMES TO SANTA FE

IN THE early morning light, hills and mountains ringed the scene, with Santa Fe on the plain. From the wagon camp, the town looked like a handful of ivory blocks spilled by a giant hand. Some blocks followed the streets in close-set rows. Others huddled anywhere at all. From taller blocks came the far-off songs of bells. The notes seemed to wing across the sage like merry birds.

The camp was busy. Water splashed in buckets. Razors flip-flapped on leather straps, and the air smelled of fancy store-soap.

'Great goats in the mountains!' moaned Buck, staring into a mirror. 'Is that *me*? Last time I saw me was Council Grove. Leapin' panthers! I've growed more hair than a buffalo bull in the Fall!'

'I know,' said Jed patiently. 'An' you want me to trim your locks an' shave your jaws, as I've done on this here hill the past eight years. So squat on that keg an' let's get the torture over with!'

Jed curried Starbright and Bugle, and buffed the brass balls on their horns. Buck helped him polish the studs and bells of the yoke until they glittered. Then, with every man dressed in his best and all boots shining, the caravan crawled like an endless snake downhill.

The huge wagons, high as haystacks, rocked past corrals of sheep, goats and burros. Ducks and pigs scrambled out of irrigation ditches and fled noisily. It was a great day for the men, eight hundred miles from Independence. It was a great day for the happy people of Santa Fe. Guns boomed, church bells rang, Spanish welcomes were shouted from doorways and flat rooftops. The train rumbled through crooked streets walled by whitewashed adobe houses. Starbright and Bugle stepped proudly, leading the caravan. And the yoke's bells jingled merrily to the open plaza, at the very center of town.

PALACE OF THE GOVERNORS

This building faces south on the old Plaza. Once it formed the south wall of a fort. Built in 1609, this Palace has been in use ever since.

When it was seventy-one years old Indians burned the rest of Santa Fe— (Revolt of 1680), drove all Spaniards from the Southwest, and used this building as a seat of government for twelve years. Then New Mexico was re-conquered for Spain.

One hundred thirty years after that (in 1822) the Mexican flag, telling the Southwest that Mexico was free from Spain, was flown from the Palace. And here General Kearny (in 1846) took possession for the United States.

Today this ancient Palace is a museum of Southwest history— a history that has flamed, yelled, thundered and slept around its adobe walls for almost three and a half centuries.

THE plaza was the very heart of the West. Yet it was nothing but a big square of bare ground. Not a blade of grass, a flower or a tree grew here. Water for man and beast ran in ditches on two sides. It was surrounded by churches and homes of wealthy citizens. On the north side stood the Palace of the Governors. This long, low adobe building with its row of log pillars did not look much like a palace, yet it had housed every governor since New Mexico was born. It had weathered Indian battles and fire, and was one of the oldest relics of the early Spaniards. It was even one year older than the wood of the yoke.

Trade went on briskly around this plaza. Even some of the caravan animals would be traded off. Oxen, needed for high-wheeled carts in New Mexico, would be bartered for mules wanted back in Missouri. But not Starbright and Bugle. Just now all the beasts were performing their last work before going to green pastures. They tugged and backed the creaking wagons until they framed the open square, hub to hub.

For days the prairie schooners remained here while calico, laces, glassware, gunpowder, hardware and fancy goods changed hands. New Mexican merchants bought whole wagonloads of supplies for their shops in Taos and other towns. The square was a moving patchwork quilt of brightest colors. Rich ladies and gentlemen stalked through the plaza. So did Mexican soldiers in uniform and officers heavy with gold braid. Ordinary people crowded this open-air market by hundreds. Poor people flocked to look at trinkets, if not to buy. And blanketed Indians from the near-by pueblos stood staring at these magic things from a world beyond.

27. END OF THE TRAIL

Thus the cottonwood yoke came to the end of the Trail. Now it hung in state from the front of Jed's wagon. Many people came to examine it.

Among them was a beautiful young lady. Jed knew this Spanish girl. To him she was a young sapling, straight and slender. Her hair, black and glossy as a raven's wing, held a high comb. A white lace mantilla draped over the comb, framing her face in a foaming waterfall. Her eyes, Jed thought, were like deep pools in a forest — one moment shadowy-dark, and very still — the next sparkling with sunbeams. But at last she took her eyes from his gaze, and stepped to the wagon.

'Ah, Meester Jed,' she said softly, stroking the yoke with slender hands. 'These are the bells I gave you last year when you came. Please tell me the story of this yoke I have heard so much about!'

'Well now,' began Jed, still staring, but not at the yoke.

'Aw, he's bashful an' tongue-tied, Miss,' drawled Buck. 'His seein' you is like sightin' a cool spring in a desert. Or like comin' on a warm campfire after a blizzard. Both at once, sort of, if you know what I mean. So set on this keg till he catches his breath, an' I'll spin you the yarn. . . .'

The merry people of Santa Fe liked the Americanos. They gave a fiesta in honor of the caravan. Days were filled with races, games, music and wonderful food. Guitars strummed in the moonlit nights, fiddles sang, Spanish slippers and Missouri boots tapped the floors endlessly. Buck danced with two dozen different girls, one after the other. But Jed danced only with the girl of the silver bells.

ONE day, years afterward, two horsemen stopped at a house in Santa Fe. A dark-eyed lady peered through a window, gasped, and disappeared. A man dashed from the house, pulling one of the strangers from his saddle.

'Buck!' cried Jed, holding the dusty traveler in a bear hug. 'Maria and I haven't seen you for three winters! What have you been up to? Are you married yet?'

'Married?' snorted Buck. 'Nope, I'm too wild and woolly to settle down like you did! I been roamin' the far spaces, as usual. An' I've brung along a Kansas Injun who wants to clap eyes on the yoke afore he dies. Many-Eagles, here's Jed Simpson, best cabinet-maker in New Mexico!'

That evening Maria sat in a high-backed Spanish chair. The three men squatted on buffalo robes on the floor. Smoke from their pipes lifted above the fireplace, where the yoke hung on polished antlers.

'Long time past,' spoke Many-Eagles in his soft Kansas tongue, 'my ancestor saved a young sapling. He became a great Medicine Man, the first of many in my family. When I was a boy, my father said "the Medicine-Tree will some day travel from its hill." I did not know how this could be. Then I, too, became a Medicine Man.... Now my eyes see what will come before it comes.... I see the buffalo gone from the open plains; many farms and fences where they roamed; great trails, with wagons rolling on them, not pulled by animals; giant Thunderbirds roaring through the skies....

'Too many things I see, for you to understand. But this you will understand —' and he looked long at Jed, and at Maria, his wife. 'The Good-Medicine still lives in this yoke. Keep it always. It will bring peace to your lodge....'

THE END

AN INDIAN PICTUI STORY OF TH TREE

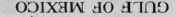

GULF OF MEXICO

ATLANTIC OCEAN

SANTA FE TRAIL 1834

THE RED LINE SHOWS WHERE THE SANTA FE TRAIL USED TO BE

THE DARK GREEN AREA SHOWS EASTERN FORESTS AT THE TIME OF THE TREE

LIGHT GREEN SHOWS PRAIRIES AND PLAINS OF LONG GRASS

TAN SHOWS THE HIGHER, ARID PLAINS OF SHORT BUFFALO GRASS

WEST OF THESE PLAINS RISE HIGH PLATEAUS, AND THE SNOW-CAPPED RANGES OF THE ROCKY MOUNTAINS. MOST OF THESE MOUNTAIN SLOPES WERE THICKLY FORESTED.

NAMES OF INDIAN TRIBES SHOW WHERE THEY ONCE LIVED

MAIN RIVERS OF THIS STORY ARE SHOWN IN BLUE

MANY CARGOES OF TRADE GOODS WERE SHIPPED TO THE WEST BY WAY OF THE MISSISSIPPI AND MISSOURI RIVERS FROM THE OLD FRENCH CITY OF

New Orleans

TRIBES OF THE SOUTHEASTERN WOODLANDS

INDIAN

MISSISSIPPI

QUAPAW TRIBE

MISSOURI TRIBE

OHIO RIVER TRADE ROUTE TO THE SOUTH AND EAST

St. Louis FOUNDED BY THE FRENCH—THE ORIGINAL STARTING POINT OF SANTA FE TRAIL.

...anklin

...E STARTING ...INT FOR ...NTA FE TRAIL ...S AT

TRIBES OF THE EASTERN WOODLANDS

Cincinnati

Pittsburgh

TRADE GOODS FROM EASTERN STATES WERE SHIPPED DOWN THE OHIO RIVER

INDIAN

Chicago— ONCE FORT DEARBORN

LAKE MICHIGAN

Detroit

AN OLD FRENCH FORT

LAKE ST. CLAIR

LAKE ERIE

NOV   2007

J   Holling, Holling
HOL   Clancy.

          Tree in the trail.

$11.95

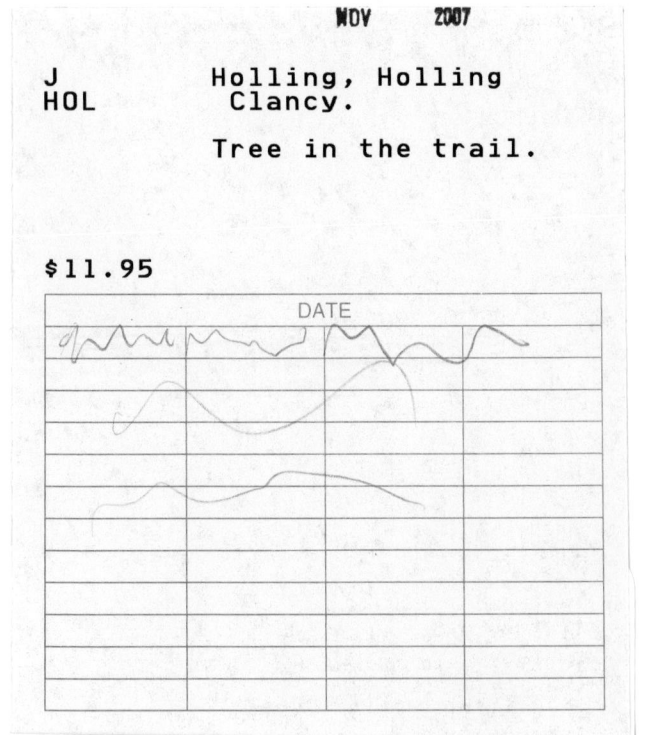

DATE			

BAKER & TAYLOR